HOT LESBIAN EROTICA

La Chatte Noire

THE LAURA AND SHONTAY CHRONICLES, PART 3

Miranda Mars

WARNING

This book contains sexually explicit scenes and adult language. It may be considered offensive to some readers. This book is for sale to adults ONLY.

* * * * * * * * * * * * * * * * * * *

Please store your files wisely where they cannot be accessed by underage readers.

Please feel free to send me an email. Just know that these emails are filtered by my publisher. Good news is always welcome.

Miranda Mars - **Miranda_mars@awesomeauthors.org**

WANT FREE COPIES OF MY BOOKS?

Just visit my blog and download free copies of my books:
http://miranda-mars.awesomeauthors.org/

About the Publisher

4Fun Publishing, a member of **BLVNP Incorporated**, 340 S. Lemon #6200, Walnut CA 91789, info@blvnp.com / legal@blvnp.com
NOTE: Due to the highly emotional reaction of some people to works of erotic fiction, any email sent to the above address that contains foul language or religious references is automatically deleted by our anti-spam software and will not be seen. All other communications are welcome.

DISCLAIMER

Please don't be stupid and kill yourself. This book is a work of FICTION. Do not try any new sexual practice that you find in this book. It is fiction and not to be confused with reality. Neither the author nor the publisher or its associates assume any responsibility for any loss, injury, death or legal consequences resulting from acting on the contents in this book. Every character in this book is over 18 years of age. The author's opinions are not to be construed as the opinions of the publisher. The material in this book is for entertainment purposes ONLY. Enjoy.

The Laura and Shontay Chronicles, Part 3

La Chatte Noire

Hot Lesbian Erotica

By: Miranda Mars

© **Miranda Mars 2015**
ISBN: 978-1-68030-321-6

There was an uncomfortable shock in store for Laura.

She was in ninth heaven after her night with Arthell, which helped to cushion the blow a little, though not much. While lying in bed with Sara on Friday night, in Sara's apartment, tired and happy after an hour of intensely sweet and tender fucking, Sara grew solemn. Tracing an invisible line down Laura's cheek with one finger, her dark eyes wide and limpid, she asked,

"Would you hate me if I did this with another woman?"

When Laura, who was floored by the totally unexpected question, failed to answer right away, Sara went on. She even kissed Laura's mouth, half-open with awe and shock, first.

"Don't be upset," she whispered. "It wouldn't mean I didn't love you. I know how upset you were when Evangelina paid me that visit. Even though she and I are old friends. You see it didn't affect the way I feel about you." Sara's fingertip made a curve under Laura's chin and up her other cheek. "And I know you haven't been exactly . . . how shall we put it . . . chaste? I don't mean just Dee Dee. But I'm not blind. I can sense when you've been . . . you know, sniffing some other chick's crotch."

She made one of her devastatingly funny faces, which, in spite of her stunned silence, made Laura laugh. It was a gesture that made it absolutely impossible for Laura to lie and protest that Sara's accusation was not true. She considered it the better part of discretion to remain silent.

But when Sara did not go on, Laura said, "I wouldn't hate you. I would never hate you."

"I hope you mean it," Sara said softly.

"Why. Have you done it already?"

Sara shook her head, looking suddenly very innocent and shocked to be suspected. "Only with Lina. I mean, Evangelina." She propped her head on her hand, gazing intently into Laura's eyes. "There's this nurse who works down at 450 Sutter, across the hall from my office. We meet in the hallways, in the elevator, down at the snack shop, you know. She's been sort of, well, you know, coming on to me. It's kind of getting under my skin, if you know what I mean."

Laura nodded sympathetically, not knowing what else to do. She was both pained and fascinated by Sara's account of this attraction. "And you want to give her the green light? See what happens?"

Wide-eyed, Sara slowly nodded. "She's kind of pretty. Not as gorgeous as you are, but . . ."

"Is she white or black?" Laura blurted out before she could catch herself. "Or Latina," she quickly added, remembering Evangelina. Or 'Lina,' as Sara had just called her, revealing a level of intimacy that Laura had always expected was there but that hurt just the same when she was reminded of it.

Sara frowned, not a deep frown but a frown nonetheless. "Why? Does that matter to you?" Then she made a dopey face. "Are you that competitive, Laura?"

Laura blushed. "I . . . guess I am. Sorry."

"Lucky for you, she's a sister." Sara raised one eyebrow. "Knowing you, she'd probably turn your crank."

"Now that's not nice," Laura smiled. "She obviously turns yours."

Sara smiled mysteriously back at Laura. "I guess in a way she does."

Laura recognized this moment as a time when she could pout and turn petulant, perhaps playing on Sara's clear uneasiness at broaching this question. She decided not to do it. After all, you haven't been a saint, she reminded herself. You love her, and you know fucking with the others hasn't made you love her any less. Why shouldn't it work for her? In spite of the fact that I'm wildly, murderously jealous?

"What's her name?"

"None of your business," Sara turned away, as if to brush off this inquiry quickly.

"You mean I don't even get to know my rival's name?" Laura asked querulously, caressing Sara's bare brown shoulder. She realized she was skirting perilously close to the pouting she had foresworn.

"She is *not* your rival!" Sara said, angrily.

"I know . . . I'm sorry," Laura said, pulling her down again on the bed, running her hands hungrily all over Sara's wonderful curvaceous body, even though they had finished fucking only minutes earlier.

She realized that Sara's attraction to another woman suddenly made her somehow incredibly more desirable than ever to Laura. Her body felt suddenly new, fresh, alluringly voluptuous under Laura's fingers, her scent outrageously erotic, her skin a magnet for Laura's hungry lips. In another second, she had Sara's phenomenal breasts in both hands and was attempting to swallow one of her large, soft black nipples.

"Oh! Oh! Laura!" Sara hammered her fists on Laura's shoulders, half-laughing, half overcome by this sudden sexual attack.

"No wonder she wants this delicious body," Laura panted, slurping and sucking Sara's silky dark flesh with exaggerated lust.

"Oh honey . . . oh honey . . ." Sara panted, converting quickly from protest to participation.

Laura realized, and knew that Sara probably did too, that sudden, explosive sex was one way to veer around the dangerous and complex emotions their conversation had been inspiring in them both. In another minute they were deep into it, gasping and pumping and pinching and sucking, until both of them erupted more quickly than usual in sharp, squealing orgasms that left them exhausted and panting, oblivious to their earlier troubled sparring.

"Sometimes I can't believe you," Sara finally said, when she recovered her composure, rolling over to kiss the supine Laura's bare shoulder. "Nobody ever fucked me like you do."

Laura gave her a deadpan smile. She too leaned over and kissed Sara's phenomenal pillowy lips. "Let's just make sure we keep it that way," she murmured. "You might have an occasional dalliance, but I want to still be the champ."

"Nobody could ever replace you in my heart, Laura," Sara whispered solemnly.

But Laura could not help wondering.

She knew it was silly, but she worried anyway, until an email came at work that distracted her. It was from, of all people, Shontay Gibson.

Hi Laura, longtime no see. Coming to San Jose week of Oct. 4 to recruit for Alcatel. Staying in Radisson Suites. Can we visit? Dying to see you. It's been so long. Shontay. Write back here and let me know.

Laura felt her heart flutter and tiny hot darts raced through her pussy. It was not that Shontay was so important to her, certainly not as important as Sara. Or now, Arthell. But their relationship had been fascinating and dangerous and passionate, and Shontay, always jealous, had left to take her job in France with Alcatel without the slightest word to Laura. She had disappeared without notice and without a trace, with not so much as a fare thee well, leaving Laura to wonder what might have caused this vanishing act, and if she herself were partially to blame.

That had been about eight months ago, and Laura had heard nothing until this email. Feeling very excited, though Shontay's visit was still two weeks away, she immediately replied that she was looking forward to seeing her. She wanted to ask, What do you mean by Can we visit? She was totally in the dark about where their relationship stood. She and Shontay had gone so often from eating one another alive to frosty distance to actual spite and then back again to hot fucking that it was really hard to know where they would pick things up. At the time Shontay had vanished, they had been embroiled in a jealous spat, caused, as always, by Shontay's anger at Laura for playing around with others.

Do we pretend that didn't happen? Laura wondered. Am I going down to the San Jose Radisson to spend the night? Or just to make polite conversation?

She didn't know and was on pins and needles until the evening of the fourth, when she received a call from Shontay at home.

"Hi, I'm here, when are you coming down?"

"Oh god, Shontay, it's really you." Laura flushed, and found herself momentarily speechless. "You really are here."

"Of course I'm here," Shontay said, a little curtly. "Did you think I was lying?"

"No. No, I just had a hard time believing I was actually going to see you again."

"What's that supposed to mean?" Shontay snapped.

It was the same old Shontay, Laura realized. Very touchy, edgy, easy to ire, no matter what you might venture to say. Laura paused for a moment, hoping Shontay would hear the sound of her own sharp voice and soften a little.

"It's supposed to mean," she finally said, "that I'm dying to see you. I can come whenever it's convenient for you."

Even though it was an obvious compliment, Shontay did indeed seem to soften, as if she realized she was being a little harsh for someone who wanted to 'visit'. "I'm sorry, I'm a little frazzled from that long flight," she said. "I didn't mean to snap at you. I'm going to try to get some sleep, but I'll probably be up by two a.m. My internal clock hasn't adjusted yet."

"I'm afraid I can't come at two. I have to go to work tomorrow."

"Why don't you come down now? I know I won't be able to sleep."

Laura felt her whole being suddenly come alive. She had been tired herself, but no more. Her body suddenly perked up and almost vibrated. "I could be there in an hour or so. I don't know how exactly how long it would take to drive there."

"It shouldn't take you long. Come the back way, down 280."

"Right. Want me to bring anything? Food? Wine? Champagne?"

"You know me. I don't eat much. Wine will just make me sleepy. Just bring yourself. And bring the Laura I used to know . . . back when we had the good times. See you in a half hour or so."

Laura was positively humming as she packed a small suitcase.

This love of mine,
Goes on and on,
Though life is empty since you've gone . . .

She didn't know why this tune stuck in her brain. She certainly had never 'loved' Shontay, at least not in the way she adored Sara, or had felt such deep emotion for Deshona at one time. Or even the way she felt now, all tingly and ethereally happy, about Arthell. Shontay however had felt more strongly, she knew, since that was the source of their frequent quarrels. Life had not been exactly empty for Laura since she had gone to France, though. It had rarely been more exciting sexually, though the recent development with Sara (*that slutty nurse Sheena*, as Laura thought of it) had put a damper on it.

Still, she hummed the tune and packed in her strap-on just in case, and a small bottle of baby oil.

I cry my heart out,
It's bound to break,
Since nothing matters, let it break . . .

"Why am I singing this song?" she wondered aloud. "I've never felt happier. Even with Sara doing . . . her little thing. In a way, it makes me feel relieved since I don't have to feel guilty for being the only one doing it."

She realized she was talking to herself and promptly stopped. But she couldn't stop humming as she locked up the house and went out to the car. She hummed all the way to San Jose. *Do you know the way to San Jose? I've been away so long I may go wrong and lose my way.* She did not lose her way and arrived at the Radisson Suites in 47 minutes. Shontay was waiting for her in the lobby.

Laura was shocked. Shontay was gorgeous.

Laura knew she was pretty and had been the one to encourage Shontay to see herself that way, since Shontay had been convinced that, being tall and skinny, she was unalterably homely and unattractive. And she had dressed accordingly until Laura had persuaded her to wear silky, summery things that showed off her long but enchanting legs and her willowy figure. She had usually worn her hair too either in a tight bun behind her head or in a no-nonsense pony tail, but never down around her neck and cheeks, where it softened her somewhat angular face and made her look like an aristocratic and elegant model. Laura was continually taking down Shontay's hair, mussing it up, or asking to do so.

But here she was in the lobby, wearing a stylish peach-colored frock with a short skirt, with her lovely dark brown hair in soft billows around her head, her astonishing pale brown eyes lighting up with genuine gladness as she saw Laura approach.

"Oh god, you look so gorgeous!" Laura effused as she hugged her, inhaling Shontay's French perfume. "France must be so good for you."

Shontay giggled nervously and stepped back from Laura's embrace, as if this were too public a place for them to be doing something they would be doing behind closed doors in a few minutes. "Oh, cut the crap, Laura," she smiled. "We both know what you want."

Laura glanced around the lobby without moving her head, mainly to see if anyone had overheard this. She smiled sweetly back at Shontay. "I want to hear all about it, that's what I want. You do look gorgeous. I hope you won't deny it."

"You don't look too bad either," Shontay softened. "Still got all that hair."

Laura raised her hand to her hair self-consciously. She was still taking in the vision of Shontay's loveliness. Shontay was still almost painfully thin, and still looked like she had no breasts, though Laura knew otherwise. The flowery peach dress she wore did not allow one to appreciate the fine curve of her delicious rump, though Laura also knew it well. But her long thin legs were visible from the hem down and Laura's eyes feasted on them.

Shontay was the color, Laura had often though in the past, of pale clover honey, her skin smooth and flawless, and Laura could well recall having been locked between those long smooth legs, rubbing her cheek against them, kissing Shontay's inner thighs . . .

These thoughts were getting her aroused right there in the lobby, and she quickly pushed them to the back of her mind. Suddenly she found it a little awkward to be standing there in the lobby, not knowing what was coming next. It somehow didn't seem appropriate to her for them just to go up to Shontay's room and fuck. Assuming that was what Shontay had in mind. But it seemed too coarse and perfunctory.

"Shall we go have dinner . . . or a drink?" Laura suggested. "So you can tell me about it?"

Shontay scowled. As usual, Laura reminded herself, even when she was in the mood, Shontay had to scowl or snarl or make a sharp comment. She was very vulnerable and sweet inside, but outside she kept up her aloof, imperious, peremptory façade, which was a quality that had made her much disliked when she had worked at Laura's company. Laura wondered how Alcatel was handling the famously frosty Shontay. Maybe the French language softens her for them, she speculated. And then, she is a gorgeous black American model type; they probably go for that. Maybe it induces them to tolerate this crabby nature of hers. Or maybe she's not like that at all when she's around them. Only around me, and others like me.

Then Shontay's scowl turned mysteriously into a seductive smile. "I'm tired," she said quietly. "Let's go upstairs. We can order room service. Company's paying," she winked.

"I'd be delighted."

Shontay looked down at Laura's bag. "Planning to stay over? They might charge me extra." She winked again, clearly meaning it as a joke.

"I don't have to stay if you don't want me to," Laura said softly as they entered the elevator.

They were alone in it, and Shontay's room was on the twelfth floor. She did not answer Laura's question, letting it hang. Finally, she looked back over her shoulder as she led Laura down the hall to her room. She was grinning.

"I'll let you know."

Inside the room Laura sat on the edge of one queen-sized bed and kicked off her shoes. Shontay went over to the drapes and pulled them shut. Gosh, we aren't going to waste any time, are we, Laura thought. She realized she was very aroused. She knew Shontay, though skinny and sharp, always had this effect on her, probably because of the challenge involved in breaking through the ice layer. She was also physically lovely, though skinny. You could still be lovely while skinny. Laura's eyes lingered on the smooth, rich café-au-lait hue of Shontay's long legs.

Shontay saw her looking and smiled. "You know, I think you're the first woman who ever found me attractive," she said calmly.

"But not the last," Laura smirked knowingly.

Shontay shook her head. Her loose hair swished around her ears, making Laura's pussy flutter. "No, not the last. I've got two lovers in France. Girls. Actually, three. One guy, if you can believe it. They're wild for *la chatte noire*, as they call it."

God, I could use a little of that *chatte noire* myself right now, Laura thought, feeling very aroused, very hungry for Shontay. The new Shontay, she corrected herself. Once Laura had broken through the ice, Shontay was always eager for fucking, except when she was periodically furious with Laura over Laura's other girlfriends. But prior to Laura, she had, as she recounted it, simply given up on sex, with men of course, since Laura had been her first woman.

And now look at her. Not only gorgeous, stylish, self-assured, and sexy, but possessed of three, count them, three French lovers of both sexes.

"I'm a little wild for it myself," Laura said, unable to resist the opportunity.

"I know," Shontay said mordantly. "Black cunt."

She was alluding to one of their conversations long ago, when she had accused Laura bluntly of being overly fond of this lovely item. Hers and others'. The words 'black cunt' sounded so earthy and coarse and dirty coming from this gorgeous woman who looked like a super-model that the combination was enchanting, and Laura perceived her lust ratcheting up a few notches. Black cunt sounded so much more arousing than *la chatte noire*. Though maybe the latter sounded pretty sexy if you were French.

"You're so nasty," Laura smiled curtly. "Always so nasty and rude. You meant way more to me than . . . that."

Shontay tossed her head in an arrogant, aristocratic way she had. She pursed her lips. "I doubt it."

Laura pouted. "You didn't even tell me before you left. I had to find out from that bitch Rhonda."

Shontay looked away as if embarrassed. Laura felt a slight twinge of victory. "What did she tell you?"

Laura shrugged. "That you got a job in France. That you spoke French and had graduated from the French high school in San Francisco. I felt . . . devastated."

"Oh, right," Shontay said, with heavy scorn.

Maybe that was a little too strong, Laura realized, and as ever Shontay was quick to jump on any phoniness. "Well . . . I *was* hurt," she amended.

Shontay grinned broadly. "Poor Laura. You had to go back to the pretty airheads. Boo hoo."

"I think we are on the wrong track," Laura said, frankly, looking directly into those enchanting pale brown eyes. "I came here because I missed you. You invited me, remember? If you think all I want is *la chatte noire*, then maybe I ought to leave."

Shontay softened again, as she usually did. Laura recalled that you had to work at it constantly, but you could get her to relax and drop the shield. But Shontay was not done teasing, in her sharp sarcastic way. She didn't want Laura to leave, but she also did not want to stop baiting her.

"Oh, and you don't want me?"

"More than anything," Laura said softly.

This was such an odd change, Laura realized. She had initially had to convince Shontay that she was indeed attractive, not the gawky, spindle-shanks, skinny, awkward, angular woman she had thought herself to be, and now Shontay was acting like a very sexy and desirable woman, toying with Laura, tempting her, taunting her, and enjoying Laura's eyes on her and Laura's obvious desire enough to prolong things with agonizing skill.

Shontay crossed the room and sat next to Laura on one of the two beds. She reached up with one hand and let her fingers trail through some strands of Laura's hair. "You know," she murmured in a very low voice, almost too low to be heard, "I really love my French girls, and the guy too, but none of them can do it for me like you did, Laura."

"I thought the French were experts in love."

Shontay let her fingers caress Laura's cheek. "Maybe in love . . . but not in . . . you know . . . that word you like so much that I told you embarrasses me."

"Fucking?"

Shontay giggled and flinched. "That's the one. I think I've missed you, Laura."

Slowly, Laura pulled her backward down onto the bed, so that they were both lying half on it, with their legs still dangling over the edge. "God, I've missed you too."

"I don't want to wrinkle up this dress," Shontay said. "I'm traveling. I only have so many. And I don't trust any hotel's cleaning service."

"I know what you mean. Why don't you let me help you take it off?"

Without answering, with only a mysterious smile, Shontay slowly sat up and turned her back to Laura. There were four buttons on her dress, which Laura unbuttoned, starting at the top. As each button came loose, and the thin fabric of Shontay's dress sagged away from her flesh, Laura kissed her smooth light brown skin, holding up Shontay's hair with one hand so that she could reach the nape of her neck with her lips.

Shontay shivered a little. She raised her own hand to her hair and held it up so that Laura could continue.

"I could kiss your marvelous back forever," Laura whispered, continuing with the buttons.

Shontay was not wearing a bra but an ivory-colored thin camisole, where Laura's lips had to stop, even though there were two buttons left. But she was content for the moment. She was a great lover of naked backs, or near-naked ones, and Shontay's was enchanting, even if

Laura had to stop momentarily halfway down. True, the wings of her shoulder blades protruded a little, and the knobs of her spine were a little more visible than most, a feature Shontay herself would consider 'bony.'

Maybe her back had a little less flesh on it than many others, but it was the color of pale honey, silky and smooth, and had a lot of seductive cambers and indentations and dips and protuberances to kiss and tenderly suck, and even though inhibited from going lower for the moment, Laura's lips were busy visiting them all.

Shontay was enjoying it too. "Oh god . . . that feels good," she sighed, bending her head forward a little to give Laura full access to the nape of her neck again.

Laura took advantage of the opportunity and licked and sucked the skin sensually. She then kissed the slightly raised nub of each vertebra on her way again down Shontay's back to the edge of the camisole. Meanwhile, she was unbuttoning the last two buttons. Shontay's dress now gaped open, and Laura could reach the bottom of the camisole with her fingers.

"Here . . . let's take this off," she murmured, pushing the top half of the loose dress down Shontay's arms, then lifting up the camisole, with Shontay's help.

Shontay turned to face her as the camisole went up over her head. When it came free, she was naked from the waist up. Laura's hands were already covering the marvelous little teacup breasts that she remembered so well. Her mouth came close to Shontay's, then pressed into it, and they were kissing hungrily.

Shontay's long arms encircled Laura, and her fingers plucked at the fabric of Laura's shirt. "Take this off," she breathed into Laura's lips.

Laura pulled back, smiling. "Let's take everything off."

Shontay shook her head. "No. A little bit at a time. More exciting that way. The way you used to do it." She watched while Laura unbuttoned her shirt, removed it, then removed her black lace bra too. "Remember when we were fighting . . . and you pushed your mouth into my panties? Pushed my panties up into my . . ."

Laura waited, still smiling. "Your pussy? Can't you say that? Your *chatte*? You're beautiful *chatte noire*?"

Shontay looked down, in genuine embarrassment. It was such a thrill for Laura to see her like this since she was always so sharp and imperious. She did have a streak of genuine vulnerability which was however hard to reach. But this moment also reminded Laura how Shontay had quickly become much more emotionally invested in their relationship than Laura had been, which had caused their frequent hostilities.

"Let me feel you," Laura whispered, holding out her open arms again. "It's been so long."

Shontay nodded slowly, leaning forward, coming into Laura's outstretched arms. Now their naked breasts touched at the same time their mouths met, and they melted together into a lengthy, sensual kiss, moving their half-naked bodies together so that they could feel every last bit of pleasure from their skins touching, their breasts rubbing together, their hardening nipples kissing too.

Laura ran her fingers now up and down the whole supple length of Shontay's marvelous long back, feeling the smooth skin that had formerly been concealed by the camisole, wanting to kiss it, feeling the sexual pressure build inside her body, surprised by the physical desire she had for this thin, complicated girl.

"Mmmm, I want to kiss this incredible back forever," she purred, rubbing the warm, smooth skin and long resilient muscles. "Lie down and let me rub and kiss your back."

Obediently, Shontay quickly shed the rest of her frock, wriggling out of it and tossing it across the room onto a chair. She still had on her ivory bikini panties, which matched her camisole. She stretched out on her stomach, looking dreamily back over her shoulder as Laura began making love to her back.

There was no other word for it. Laura loved this honey gold masterpiece. Now that Shontay was completely naked, except for her panties, Laura could explore, caress, and kiss it to her heart's content. She began by slipping out of her own skirt so that she too was wearing only her panties, then straddling Shontay's long, thin thighs with her own and massaging the firm flesh on each side of Shontay's neck, starting gently, squeezing the muscles, then doing it a little harder, until Shontay was gasping and moaning.

"Oh god, I love your back . . ." Laura murmured, bending close, letting her own naked breasts sweep across the flesh of Shontay's back as she pressed her lips to the firm flesh she had been rubbing. "I love your body. I missed this long thin body so much."

Shontay was sighing and moaning almost unconsciously. Her eyes fluttered open and she smiled drowsily. "You liar," she sighed softly. "If you keep this up, I'll fall asleep and there won't be any fun."

Laura leaned up a little further so that her lips could reach Shontay's ear. Her breasts now mashed more forcefully into Shontay's naked back, and she slithered her tongue into the marvelous molasses-colored whorl. "There's going to be fun you wouldn't believe, darling," she breathed. "You didn't know I'm the jealous type. I'm going to put those French girls in the shade."

Shontay shivered and giggled throatily and writhed a little under Laura's body.

"And if you fall asleep, I know just how to wake you up."

"I'll bet you do," Shontay smiled.

She tried to turn and get up to face Laura, but Laura was having none of it. "I'm not finished. Lie still. I haven't even got down half of this incredible back."

For the next five minutes Laura explored every silky inch of tawny, honey-colored flesh on Shontay's back, working from the top to the bottom, kissing and rubbing and stroking Shontay's long, smooth muscles, until her lips finally reached the wonderful shallow dimples above the girl's delicious, up-jutting bottom. For a tall, thin woman, Shontay had, as Laura had remarked in the past, a spectacular ass. Apart from her singular aloof and imperious beauty, the first thing Laura had noticed about Shontay was this magnificent little rump, which had been clearly visible in its outlines even under the drab, severe business pants suits Shontay had always worn until Laura persuaded her to give them a rest.

It was high and firm and out-curved, the way Laura loved them, not large, not pendulous, but a high, tight little butt that Laura just ached to kiss, stroke, and bite. And now she had an opportunity again to do just that. She knew it had driven Shontay wild in the past, and she intended for history to repeat itself.

"I love your ass," she murmured, pulling Shontay's panties down to reveal it. "God, I love your ass."

Shontay said nothing but squirmed a little with her hips to lift her ass up even more, knowing how besotted Laura always was with it. Laura had pulled Shontay's panties halfway down her thighs and decided now just to take them completely off. She kissed the upper slopes of Shontay's buns while doing it, then flung them off the bed and passionately attacked Shontay's beautiful bottom for real, squeezing and sucking and kissing Shontay's firm golden cheeks until Shontay was gasping and wriggling.

"Oh . . . oh . . . oh god, Laura . . . oh god that feels so good . . . oh yesssss!"

"I love your ass," Laura panted. "And I love your sweet pussy . . ."

She couldn't keep her hand off it. Even though she was mouth-mauling Shontay's beautiful ass, she dipped one hand under it and rubbed the wet, swollen lips of Shontay's pussy with the tips of all her fingers. Shontay undulated under her caresses, panting more and more uncontrollably. Suddenly, she twisted her body and sat up, forcing Laura to the side, so that they were again face to face.

"You . . . don't get to have all the fun . . ." she panted, her marvelous pale brown eyes fiery and glazed.

"I thought you *were* having fun," Laura teased.

Shontay grabbed her forcefully and pulled Laura down on the bed with her. "I am. I want you too. I didn't call you up just so you could . . . do that. I want some too. I want your body too."

Laura smiled warmly at her. "So nice to be wanted. I suppose you want me to get out of these."

She pointed to her own panties as she slid them down off her legs. Shontay watched intently, then purposely put her hand between Laura's thighs, as Laura had done to her, a shocking gesture from the usually shy and somewhat inhibited girl. The new Shontay, Laura thought. Aggressive. Knows what she wants.

"That's better," Shontay murmured, still touching Laura's wet pussy, but with her other arm encircling Laura's neck, bringing her face close for another hot, wet tongue kiss.

They started slowly, kissing sensually and rubbing each other's pussy gently, though insistently, but the heat level slowly grew until they were groping harder and sucking each other's lips, clanking teeth, panting and mewling. Both were so wet and aroused that Laura wondered how either one could last another minute. She herself was notoriously quick to come at a moment like this, the first time, when they had both just got naked and were groping and sucking and rubbing together. But Shontay was different—or at least she had been in the past—and rarely came quickly or easily.

At the moment, however, it seemed like she might come at any second. Low, helpless gurgles of sexual excitement came from deep in her throat as Laura massaged her swollen, greasy cunt with two fingers, swirling them over Shontay's clit, which she knew was a tiny pinkish jewel and still hidden under its protective hood. Laura had sucked and tongued this pussy she was rubbing so many times in a rapture of wild sexual worship that she knew it well, and was loving the process of getting reacquainted.

"Unhh! Ungghrrrmmm!" Shontay half-growled, her body sagging momentarily in Laura's embrace.

But even though they both seemed to be close, there was always a part of Laura that didn't want it to happen fast. She loved holding Shontay's thin, angular, naked body against hers. She loved the feel of Shontay's small but very firm breasts pushing into her own excited flesh, and she was hungry to get her mouth once again on those marvelous quarter-sized dark caramel nipples. She wanted to taste the wonderful flavors of this delicious small slit she was now rubbing heatedly. She knew there would be time, there would be time enough for all of this, but she somehow wanted it all now, as usual succumbing to her impossible desires, her need to consume and ingest and inhale her present lover.

"Unhh! Ungghrrrmmm!" Shontay groaned again, this time a little more desperately.

"Oh god . . . honey . . . I think I might come!" Laura gasped into her cheek, letting her mouth fall to Shontay's bare shoulder, nipping it lightly in her frenzy.

Shontay was similarly overcome but not so lost that she couldn't smile mysteriously down at Laura and move her hand more swiftly in Laura's crotch. "Good," she panted, "do it."

"Ohhhnnngggg!" Laura gasped, feeling it arrive whether she wanted it yet or not. "Oh god . . . unngghhhh . . . aauunnnggghhhh! Mnnnnggggauugghhnnn!"

She couldn't stop herself and came in a quick, wrenching spasm that threw her body off balance so that she fell to the mattress, pulling Shontay down with her, straining and shuddering through the last few jolts. Miraculously, her hand was still fastened to Shontay's pussy, and she rubbed it again excitedly.

"Want you to come too . . ." she gasped into Shontay's shoulder. "Want you to come."

"Oh!" Shontay gasped, thrusting with her hips. "Oh . . . unnnn! Laura . . . yes!"

"Are you there?"

"Oh! Oh . . . almost," Shontay grimaced, pumping hard, her fingers biting into Laura's arm. "Unnngghh!" she groaned, her face contorted, her body hard and tense.

For some reason, Laura was flooded with a fresh influx of sexual frenzy, probably from knowing that she was about to make Shontay come. There was a shiny spot of her own spittle left between Shontay's wonderful honey-gold shoulder and her neck, left there when Laura had bitten it just before coming herself. She immediately opened her mouth and sucked this piece of Shontay's flesh back into it, sliding two fingers up into Shontay's inflamed wet pussy and fucking her frantically with them. Next she sucked her way up to Shontay's long, smooth, aristocratic neck, then to her earlobe, which she nipped lustfully.

"Oh god, I love to fuck you!" she whispered, remembering how dirty talk had always ignited Shontay's most violent orgasms.

Shontay's thin, long, flexing thighs clenched a little, and her body jumped in a sharp spasm. "Anngghiiee!" a tight squeal escaped from her throat.

Laura, knowing she was coming, pinned her to the bed, rolling on top of her and hand-fucking her relentlessly. Another hard flinch, and then Shontay went into quick, spastic convulsions, whinnying softly deep in her chest. Her long, angular body undulated under Laura's, and her muscles contracted in a rolling rhythm of quick orgasmic fluttering.

"Oh! Ohhnnnnnnn! Ohnnnnnn . . . god, Laura, god . . . ohhnnnnnnn!" she moaned, clenching, sighing and gurgling for a long minute, then coming out of it almost as quickly as Laura had come out of her own climax.

Laura's had been quick and explosive, while Shontay's had been rolling thunder, but both were humbled and stunned by the aftermath, and they melted together effortlessly, sighing and laughing softly and stroking each other as the sweet waning spasms died away. Laura kissed her neck again, and her shoulder, and licked them both, unable to get enough of this rich, smooth, tawny golden skin.

"My, that was quick," she murmured, still half-breathless, into Shontay's delicious, silky, honey-colored throat.

"I think it was a record for me," Shontay grinned, also panting softly, kissing Laura back on her forehead. She yawned. "You'll have to forgive me if I fall asleep. Long flight. Jet lag."

"I'll bet I can keep you awake," Laura nuzzled her, dropping her face down Shontay's smooth upper chest to her marvelous little teacup breasts, which she was not going to deprive herself of any longer. "For a while, at least."

Shontay smiled drowsily, watching Laura's tongue snake out to lick one of her beautiful bulging caramel nipples. "I forgot how you like to rut and rut."

"You mean fuck and fuck?"

"Whatever. Ohhhhnnnn . . . god, that feels good. Do the other one too?"

"Mmmm, like this?"

"Yesss!"

Laura treasured these beautiful little mounds and made love to them both with exquisite skill, licking and tonguing Shontay's dark, thick nipples, then sucking and even nipping them, until they were stiff and rubbery and wet and shiny like dark plums, darker now that she had been sucking them and drawing blood into them. She slid up to kiss Shontay again while pinching Shontay's wet nipples with her fingers, scissoring them lightly, twisting them, squeezing the girl's small breasts and slithering her tongue deep into Shontay's mouth.

"Are you going to let me fuck you again before you fall asleep?" she teased, nibbling Shontay's earlobe. "You love it when I talk dirty to you, don't you."

"Oui, mademoiselle," Shontay smiled sexily, drowsily. "I love it when you 'fuck' me . . . and also when you tell me you're going to 'fuck' me."

As always, Shontay was very skittish about using the 'F' word and isolated it playfully from the rest of her words for Laura's benefit. "Baise-moi," she said, saucily, looking as if she might blush, if only she were pale enough to blush. "Baise-moi vite."

"Oh god," Laura erupted in soft laughter, "am I getting my French lesson for today? Mademoiselle Dupin, my tenth grade French teacher, would never let us use that word. Anyway, doesn't it mean 'kiss'? Kiss me?"

Shontay gave her a salacious smile. "It means kiss me and fuck me."

"You know," Laura said, "I brought along a little surprise. I don't know if you'll go for it . . . but . . ."

She hopped off the bed in a fit of happiness and enthusiasm. Shontay was so different: so receptive, still a little sharp, it was true, but mainly sweet and sensual and beautiful and relaxed with Laura. Was this what having three French lovers could do for you?

Laura popped across the room to her small overnight bag and extracted the strap-on dildo. She had not brought the Double Penetrator, feeling that was a little overboard for a woman to whom she had never even broached the subject of a strap-on before. Just the single ridged brown beauty that could take you to paradise when fastened to the right person.

Shontay looked at it with wry curiosity as Laura returned to the bed with it. "Oh god, I can't believe it. You really have one of those. Excuse me, I *can* believe it."

Laura presented it, so that Shontay could run her fingertip along the ridges. "This will make you die, honey."

Shontay gave her a quizzical look. "Are you going to use that on me?"

This was not the way Laura would have put it herself, and Shontay's attitude suddenly made her feel chagrined. She pulled back the dildo slowly, winding the harness straps around it as if she were preparing to put it back. "Not . . . necessarily," she stammered. "I mean . . . of course not if you don't want to."

Shontay realized that she had somehow embarrassed Laura. In the past she might have gloried in this opportunity for scorn, but now she was more pliant and warm. "Let me see it again."

She held out her hand. Laura put the dildo, wrapped in the harness straps, into it. Shontay unwrapped it and caressed it again, this time more fascinated than semi-appalled. "You know . . ." she said, almost hesitantly, as if she were being careful not to hurt Laura's feelings. "Like I told you, I have this guy in France. Named Michel. He . . . you know . . . does me like that. Whenever I let him. It isn't really what I was looking for with you."

Laura smiled and reached out to take the dildo back. "I understand perfectly," she said. "It was only a thought. Shoot, I just enjoy kissing you. And pushing my body against yours. I don't need this thing. It was just a passing idea."

She crossed the room and put it back into her small bag. When she returned, Shontay had uncoiled her long, lanky, thin, and to Laura gorgeous light brown body, so that she was stretched out full length across the bed, from top to bottom, propping her head on one hand, smiling at Laura in a mysterious way, her phenomenal pale brown eyes flecked with glowing embers of sex that Laura remembered seeing there in the past. Her hair, earlier in soft billows around her head and cheeks, was now mussed and askew and fluffed out, making her look wildly sensual and fiercely desirable to Laura.

"Let me tell you something," Shontay murmured, as Laura rejoined her on the bed, stretching out to face her, but scooting up too, since Shontay was about four inches taller than she was. "You know what I keep remembering? That time when we did it in my Daddy's armchair. Remember that?"

"How could I ever forget it," Laura rolled her eyes up. "I don't think I've ever had such a hot experience."

Shontay laughed. "Me either. I couldn't look at that chair after-ward. Every time I would visit them, I'd just have to keep from looking at it. Or if I were there alone, feeding Willie [her parents' cat], I'd just act like it didn't exist. You know, make wide circles around it, while looking up at the ceiling. I was afraid if I looked at it, I start creaming my panties, or panting, or whimpering, or something."

Laura leaned forward and kissed her, a long, romantic, tongue-entangling kiss. "Do you feel like you want to do that again?" she whis-pered.

Without answering, Shontay let her eyes drift across the large hotel room to the easy chair by the window. It was a taut, upholstered maroon chair with sturdy thick arms. The instant Laura saw it she real-ized that it might be even better for the purpose than Mr. Gibson's worn overstuffed monster where they had first done this.

"I'm only afraid I'll scream so loud that the hotel staff will try to break in to save me," Shontay confessed charmingly.

"Mmmm, we can probably come up with a solution for that," Laura said, scooting forward as she kissed her again, so that she could feel the entire length of their naked bodies pressing together, a sensation that always made her head suddenly light.

Now that she knew their ultimate destination, Laura could take her time. She knew what Shontay wanted, she knew where they would end up, but for the moment she could take her pleasure with Shontay's marvelous, smooth, slender body. Shontay rarely came quickly anyway, and certainly not the second time, so that Laura could make the most of this opportunity and bring the girl to the absolute brink before dragging her across the room to the chair for a final loving rape.

"Are you going to let me suck your beautiful pussy first?" Laura murmured against her soft light brown cheek. "Such a beautiful pussy . . . your little *chatte noire*, and you waste it all on those lucky French girls and that guy Michel, when here I am dying for it . . . dying to slide my tongue right up into it . . ."

While she was murmuring softly to Shontay, she was also descending with her mouth and hands down the girl's long, angular, naked body, nuzzling her flesh, sucking her dark caramel nipples again, still descending, kissing every inch of Shontay's long midriff, every silky soft ridge of long muscle, every inch of smooth, downy skin, every rise of surfacing rib, until her lips reached the upper edge of Shontay's raven-black pubic patch, which she felt bristling against her chin. The ripe, musky perfumes of Shontay's aroused cunt filled her nostrils.

During this slow descent, Shontay sighed and twisted, growing more aroused the lower that Laura went, knowing her ultimate goal, knowing that this was only preliminary to Laura's mouth on her pussy, driving her to new heights of need. She said nothing but looked down her long body at Laura's mouth on her flesh, at Laura's tongue burrowing into her navel, at Laura's fingers gently pinching and kneading her erect nipples.

"Ohhhnnnn! Unhhhhh! Ungghh!" she finally groaned as Laura's lips reached the swollen, spreading petals of her gaping pussy.

As Laura now remembered, though everything about Shontay was long—her arms, her legs, her waist, her glorious back, her entire body—and her skin was the color of pale sage honey, her pussy lips were actually very black, and her pussy itself was small, not long at all, a snug little glistening magenta slot, all juicy and wet inside, her labia swollen and gaping. Laura wasted no time in pouring her worship all over it.

She sucked and tongued and licked it for about five minutes, at first going slowly, not wanting to accelerate Shontay's arousal too quickly, instead letting it percolate and simmer, avoiding Shontay's clit until the later stages. Finally, with her thumbs she spread open the small hood concealing the magic bead, which in Shontay's case was tiny but extremely sensitive. Laura licked it carefully, watching Shontay's face as the girl grimaced with pleasure and whimpered.

"Unnhhhh! Oh! Unnhhhh . . . oh Laura!"

"Mmmm, I don't want you to come yet . . . because I'm going to fuck you in the chair. Remember?" Laura murmured softly to her, taking great care now not to arouse her past the breaking point, though she knew it was unlikely Shontay would come too fast.

But this calculation proved to be premature. After passionately licking and sucking Shontay's small, beautiful pussy for three or four minutes she realized that Shontay was getting close, very close, far closer than she had expected. Shontay whimpered, mewling softly and help-lessly, her hips swirling, her pelvis occasionally quaking, her fingers flut-tering around her nipples, then twisting them absently as she gasped, her bleary eyes rolling upward. Laura could recognize the signs, and the last thing she wanted—and she knew the last thing Shontay wanted—was for her to come before they got over to the chair. There were, after all, a finite number of orgasms they could have, especially when Shontay was so exhausted and jet lagged, and they both yearned for that one.

Laura pulled back, not abruptly, not wishing to disturb the flow of Shontay's increasingly urgent sexual rhythms, but slowly, kissing her tense thighs, then her smooth, flat belly, sliding upward until she held her and they were face to face.

"Come with me, ma cherie," she murmured to her, kissing her cheek, her ear. "Come with me to the chair. Laura is going to fuck your pretty pussy to heaven."

Shontay's lovely pale brown eyes were glazed, her breath coming quickly, her mouth slack, but she managed a wry smile. "Oui . . . made-moiselle," she said, her eyelids heavy, quickly sitting up and following Laura off the bed as Laura pulled her by the hand.

They crossed the room to the chair, which Laura tugged out a lit-tle from the wall to make it more accessible.

"Laura . . . I'm going to scream. I know I am," Shontay said again. "I'm so damned horny, even after that first one. God, you got me all worked up, girl."

"Don't worry about a thing, darling," Laura reassured her, turning her and placing her in the chair. "I'm going to kiss you so hard you can scream right into my mouth. No one will hear a thing but me. And I *want* to hear it."

Since they had done this before, though months earlier, Shontay knew how to place herself, and Laura only had to assist her. Shontay lay back in the chair at nearly a forty-five degree angle, with her magnificent tight little rump perched on the very edge of the cushion, her lovely small black pussy splayed and inflamed and upturned, the wet red inner flesh raw and shiny with juices. Her amazingly long legs she propped over the arms, spreading her thighs so widely that it was the easiest thing in the world for Laura to climb on top of her and straddle the arms of the chair with her own thighs, also spreading her own groin enough for her throbbing cunt to press directly down onto Shontay's.

The sensation of their wet, warm, raw inner cunt flesh touching sent them both into temporary paroxysms of sexual pleasure.

Shontay stiffened and shuddered a little. "Unhhhhh! Oh shit . . . oh merde!" she giggled. "I forgot how good that feels."

Laura leaned forward and placed both hands on the back of the chair, remembering how this gave her almost ferocious leverage for fucking. This could be sweet, could be gentle, but it was likely to be fierce and explosive instead, as it had been last time. After they had done it in Shontay's father's chair, Shontay had accused Laura, though playfully, of having raped her. She had of course enjoyed the entire ride, and she appeared to be enjoying this one too.

"Unhh! Unhhh!" she grunted softly as Laura, now beginning to move her body up and down, slid her pussy across Shontay's slippery, gaping little slit.

"Ohhnngg!" Laura groaned, throwing back her head.

She too had forgotten the sheer intensity that this position could summon. With her arms extended over Shontay's head, her hands gripping the back of the chair, her naked breasts swished in Shontay's face. Shontay's hands quickly came up to them, as she had done their first time, squeezing Laura's breasts and immediately feeding one of Laura's aching nipples into her mouth. She sucked it hungrily.

"Auunngghh!" Laura half-growled, hissing with sharp pleasure. "Oh yes!"

For a brief few seconds which seemed elongated and stretched out into long minutes, they slowly moved their wet pussies together while Shontay sucked Laura's nipple as well as a large chunk of Laura's small breast entirely into her mouth, holding it there while they rocked slowly together, their hips gyrating in perfect union, slowly and patiently and relentlessly. Oh god, it's going to be even better than the first time! Laura thought wildly, feeling her body course and throb with fire and complete yearning for this magnificent, thin, and temperamental woman.

She buried her face in Shontay's frazzled, fluffed up hair, inhaling the clean, sweet odor of her scalp, gasping as she felt the slippery flesh of their cunts sliding together, intermingled with their tangled crotch hair, their clits occasionally rubbing in a way that made them both wince.

"Ungghhhh . . . oh god . . . I forgot how much I love to fuck you, Shontay . . ." Laura panted, pushing her tingling breast hard into Shontay's face. "Suck it hard. Harder!"

Shontay, while groaning and whimpering as Laura jammed her cunt into her crotch rhythmically, was also making sloppy, wet, sucking sounds as she slurped and mouth-mauled Laura's nipples, and somehow these wonderfully obscene noises ratcheted up Laura's lust to an even higher notch. Her nipples were on fire, and she even dropped one hand from the top of the chair to Shontay's head, pulling it from behind, forcing Shontay's mouth even harder into her breast.

"Bite it . . ." she gasped, losing control briefly, consumed by the fiery urge to obliterate them both in a volcanic uprush of coming. "Oh yes . . . auunngghhh!"

Shontay would bite, but never very hard, as Laura knew. She let her teeth sink a little more into Laura's throbbing nipple, then a little more, and Laura suddenly realized that if they kept this up she herself was going to come in seconds. Just in response to Shontay's teeth she was rearing and gurgling and digging her fingers into Shontay's silky flesh, groaning and at the same time fighting back the surging waves of an inevitable orgasm.

Oh no! Not so fast . . . not so fast! she told herself, wrenching herself back into self-control, slowing the pace dramatically.

"Oh noooooo . . . I don't want it to be over," she moaned to Shontay, pulling her breast out of Shontay's mouth, leaning down to hastily kiss her forehead, now glowing with a thin film of sweat. "I don't want it to be over too fast!"

Shontay, eyes glazed, smiled up at her dreamily. Without replying, she began undulating her pelvis again, so that their pussies again pressed together. Her pale brown eyes held Laura's, solemn and deadly serious, as if this moment of intimacy were the only thing that mattered in the universe at this instant. Finally, she managed to control her rapid breathing enough to speak to Laura, a soft, labored gasp.

"I . . . don't . . . either," she panted.

For Laura at least, this was the point at which the emotional content of their encounter began to deepen and expand. Something about Shontay's eyes holding hers like that stirred awake in them both a recollection of the deeper, complex feelings they had once had for each other, never 'love' in any real sense, but certainly a kind of fierce attraction-repulsion that was in some ways deeper than love. In the grip of this sudden spell, they had slowed the tempo of their fucking down to a careful, patient grind, which had the advantage of making each minuscule sensation magnified and piquant, so that the slipperiness of their wet pussies sliding together now filled them both with an almost unbearably emotional as well as sexual pleasure.

For the moment Shontay had stopped sucking Laura's breasts, which however still dangled in her face. Instead, she reached up with both hands to hold them, still never letting her eyes leave Laura's. For several minutes they gyrated together, and the only sound in the room was the chuffing of their labored breathing. But their feelings seemed to throb and swell and pulse as much as their bodies, and Laura could not prevent herself from momentarily stopping their slow grind to lower her mouth to Shontay's and drink it thirstily.

It was hard to thrust while they were kissing, but Shontay started moving her hips again in the middle of the kiss, and Laura responded, gyrating back. This quickly became so arousing that they had to stop kissing, and were panting hard, but Laura's face was still close. Shontay reached up with one hand, dropping one of Laura's breasts, and spread away the filaments of Laura's hair that had become stuck to her sweaty forehead. It was a very tender gesture that wrenched Laura's heart, so frequently had they fought and snarled at each other in the past.

"Are you going to 'fuck' me, mademoiselle?" Shontay whispered hoarsely, her pale brown eyes now flecked with excited sparks, swirling and pulsing, as if she were not going to last much longer and was asking for the final stroke. "Baise-moi? Are you going to rape me, like before?"

Laura smiled, panting seriously now. "Is that what you want me to do?" she gasped in a hoarse whisper of her own.

Again not letting Laura's eyes leave hers, Shontay nodded slowly. "I think I'm pretty close."

"God, I know I sure am," Laura gasped, kissing her again savagely before beginning to accelerate their grinding and slow pumping.

They knew they were both heading for the same goal, and that it was very close, which encouraged them to pour it on, and they began fucking more energetically and roughly than they had up to now. Laura pushed her slippery wet pussy down sharply into Shontay's inflamed seam, grunting softly and jabbing forward with her hips, grabbing the back of the chair hard for leverage, fucking her like a man would fuck her, roughly, hungrily, demandingly, completely.

For her part, Shontay, though whimpering and mewling and definitely the one underneath, who was being the recipient of this fierce love assault, flexed her body and gyrated her cunt up into Laura's too, meeting each of Laura's thrusts with her own, gasping and groaning as their physical struggle became almost too intense for either of them to bear. Now she had both hands again on Laura's small, swirling breasts, squeezing them, then voraciously feeding Laura's nipples, first one, then the other, into her mouth, sucking them sharply, deeply.

"Unnnunnnn . . . unnnunnnnn . . ." Laura heard herself moaning, her voice sounding completely demented as she pushed her breasts into Shontay's face and rabbit-jabbed the girl's warm, runny pussy with her own oozing slit. "Ohhngg! Yesssss . . . bite it . . . yesss! Unngghh!"

"Aunngghh! Oh god . . . Laura!" Shontay gasped, her thin, angular body arching and quivering under Laura's, as if she were losing control.

"You're going to come now . . . you're going to come . . . now . . . now . . ." Laura panted deliriously to her, leaning forward, but still thrusting and pumping more wildly than ever, grunting, digging her fingers into the upholstery of the chair, jamming her cunt into Shontay's, feeling her own climax surge up inside her body. "Now . . . now . . . you're going to come now . . . NOW!"

"Yaaunngngggg!" a savage, clotted cry tore itself out of Shontay's throat.

In the space of a few seconds her long, lean body went stiff, then went crazy, flipping and jackknifing almost off the chair. Laura, who was coming herself, was barely able to keep their bodies from separating, but she did it by dropping her arms from the top of the chair and embracing Shontay with them hard, mashing their bodies together, then shuddering and undulating herself as a soaring, gushing explosion of an orgasm wracked her own flesh.

"Ohnnnnmmmnngggg! Auunggghhhhh!" Laura groaned, shaking and clenching as a supreme climax wrenched her body almost too much for her to enjoy the cataclysmic nature of Shontay's.

For a moment it sounded to her like they were giving each other a chance to yell. After Shontay's initial outburst was ripped from her throat, she went silent, except for furious gasping and panting. Her body was gripped by fierce convulsions that precluded anything but mute expressions of deep physical rapture. The first jolts of Laura's climax shook and throttled her, but soon waned enough for the agonizing groans of release that had just flowed out of her lungs to surface. As they began to die away she remembered that Shontay had feared crying out too loudly, and that she herself had promised to prevent it.

"Oh honey . . . oh honey!" she gasped, grabbing Shontay's lolling head in both hands and pushing her mouth into the girl's just as Shontay erupted in a piercing scream of ecstasy. At least it would have been piercing, Laura knew, had it issued directly into the hotel room, but instead it was blocked by her open mouth. She swallowed Shontay's screams of pleasure, and for Laura it somehow made the entire experience more intense than ever, as if she were swallowing Shontay's orgasm at the same time that it was raking and wrenching Shontay's body.

"Mmmnnggrrrrnnggghmmmnngghhbbrrr!" Shontay shrieked into Laura's mouth, her body still clenching and jackknifing as each shattering spasm of her climax ripped through her. "Aunnmmmgggh! Unnn-mmrrrggghhh!"

Just as quickly as her screams had arrived, they departed, slacking off into soft, helpless mewling. The fiercest moment was past. Since they were both having trouble breathing in this odd, bent position, and also in danger of getting muscle cramps from the violent jerking and flexing they had both been undergoing, Laura quickly pulled back and slid to the side, climbing awkwardly over one arm of the chair to give Shontay more freedom of movement.

But Shontay, though blasted and destroyed by her pulverizing orgasm, grabbed Laura's hand, looking up in a dazed, stunned way at her. "Oh no . . . don't leave me."

Laura smiled and stopped. She slid halfway back into the chair, again on top of Shontay, but pressing against her more gingerly now, and half-supporting herself on the chair arm instead of Shontay's relaxed, ravished body. "I wasn't going to leave you," she explained softly. "Just ease up so you didn't get a cramp. Or me, either."

Shontay smiled wanly. "Come here and kiss me. I don't care if I get a cramp."

Laura leaned forward and kissed her more lovingly than she believed she had ever done. The new Shontay. All hair-mussed and glassy-eyed and smiling dreamily after a stunning orgasm. Her long, smooth, light brown, angular body naked and warm against Laura's. Shontay kissed back with more emotion than before. Good thing you live in France now, darling, Laura thought, or we'd be right back into the thicket we were in before you left.

"You are so sexy," Laura whispered against her smooth cheek, "that I think I could come again if I could just lie stretched out with you on the bed. You know, before you go to sleep. I am such a greedy little pig for your beautiful body."

Ever flattered by Laura's praise of her thin, somewhat bony body, Shontay grinned and flirted. "You sure are," she laughed softly, tickled by Laura's frank lechery. "You already came twice."

"You inspire me," Laura nuzzled her long, aristocratic neck.

Slowly, they disentangled themselves and Laura helped Shontay up from the chair. Shontay began yawning before she was on her feet, raising the back of one hand to her mouth. "Okay . . . but I don't know if I can make it myself," she sighed, still half-yawning. "Two is about my limit. And I'm exhausted. You really raped me again."

Her eyes twinkled at Laura.

Laura drew her back over the bed, and they stretched out face to face on it. "I hope you don't think I forced myself on you," she teased.

Shontay smiled and caressed Laura's cheek with her fingertips. "You can rape me like that any time you get the chance," she whispered. "You know, I tried that with one of my girlfriends in France. Not the chair thing . . . but just pussy to pussy. We couldn't come. Either one of us. It was fun, though. But we couldn't come. I kept remembering, Shit, every time I did this with Laura we both came."

Laura thought about it a moment. "Maybe it has to do with the build-up. You know, how long it takes you to get there. What you do before. How wound tight you are."

"Probably," Shontay nodded. "Anyway, thanks. I really needed that. I'd been thinking about it for months."

"Me too," Laura lied. Though if she had known Shontay would reappear in her life, she might have been thinking about it, she reasoned.

"Really?" Shontay beamed.

Laura nodded. "I really missed you. I was very upset that you left without telling me."

A trace of the old scorn passed over Shontay's face. "A likely story. You were busy with that skinny teenager with the braids."

"She wasn't a teenager," Laura pouted. "I'm always perfectly legal."

"Liar!" But Shontay was smiling. In the past she would have been excoriating Laura on the spot for her various peccadilloes.

Laura pulled her naked body close again and playfully tickled her armpits. "When your hair gets all messed up like that, it just makes me want to fuck you forever," she breathed into Shontay's perfect light brown ear.

"I told you I can't come again. Too tired. But go ahead, do whatever it takes you to get off. I'm your slave for love. And lust. Just use me and let me fall asleep." She winked. "We can make it again when I wake up, which if past trips are any indication, will be about three-thirty a.m."

Laura's face fell. "You make me sound so . . . so disgusting and lecherous."

Shontay laughed, throwing back her head. "If the shoe fits . . ."

"All right, that's it. No more for you." Laura sat up and crossed her arms over her naked breasts. "I might not even be here when you wake up."

Shontay grinned and pulled Laura down next to her again. "Want to bet?"

Laura smirked and laughed, trying not to. "Kiss me, you angel," she murmured. "If you had been this nice a long time ago, the girl in the braids would never have caught my eye."

"Touché, mademoiselle," Shontay murmured back, again spreading the hair away from Laura's sticky forehead before kissing her very emotionally.

After the kiss they dozed and cuddled, and soon Shontay was actually asleep, as she had promised. Laura must have watched her for half an hour before nodding off herself.

~~The End~~

WANT FREE COPIES OF MY BOOKS?

Here is a sample from another story you may enjoy:

The Laura and Shontay CHRONICLES

Complete Series

HOT LESBIAN EROTICA

Miranda Mars

She let her finger move around to Shontay's mouth, turning it so that the knuckle slid tenderly across the girl's sensual lips. Shontay seemed hypnotized by this tenderness, which was exactly Laura's intent. She could almost feel the yearning inside the girl, fighting to get out of the ice cage that entrapped it.

Abruptly, Shontay turned her head away, then turned her whole body and walked away without a word, returning to the kitchen. Laura did not follow her. She needs to be alone with those feelings for a minute, she reasoned. Whatever they are. Laura found Willie and began stroking him, making friends. Willie purred like a love-starved tractor and rubbed the side of his head violently against Laura's hand.

After a few minutes had passed, she went into the kitchen. It was remarkable how not talking, not facing one another for a brief interval could alter the mood again. Shontay was brisk and indifferent, as if Laura had never brushed her lips with her own. Laura fell right into the mood and picked up the salad bowl, moving it to the small dining table on the other side of the counter top.

"Another glass of wine?" she asked.

Shontay smiled. It was a very different smile from any she had given Laura before, somehow more intimate, warmer. We kissed, Laura thought. It was only a little brush of the lips, but she knows we kissed. That's what she's smiling about.

She poured each of them another glass of wine. Shontay had still not moved from the kitchen toward the table. Laura waited. Shontay turned and looked at her.

"You really want to do that again?" she asked, so softly that Laura almost could not hear her.

Laura's heart fluttered. Yes!

She walked calmly around the counter and back into the kitchen. "Yes," she whispered, looking dreamily up into the electrifying pale brown eyes. "But you're so tall . . . you'll have to stoop down a little."

"I don't mind that," Shontay whispered back. "No touching, though."

"No touching," Laura shook her head.

Their eyes were locked in a pulsing connection as they brought their faces close, then closer. Shontay bent her head down slightly. Their lips brushed again, as before. As promised, Laura kept her hands at her sides, letting her lips express everything she felt. First she lightly brushed Shontay's with them as before.

Their eyes were still open, still looking at each other, though too close to really see anything but skin and facial contours. Laura could almost taste Shontay's sweet, moist breath. Shontay did little but let Laura's lips caress hers. She didn't move or blink.

Laura slowly pressed closer. She pressed her lips into Shontay's marvelously sensual mouth, tilting her head to let them curve naturally into the receptive curvature of Shontay's own lips, finally feeling a slow awakening, a responsive movement in Shontay's mouth against hers. Now they were really kissing, not flirting with it, and Laura saw Shontay's eyelids fall, feeling an almost palpable warmth that had not been there before begin to radiate between their bodies, which were still separated by about six inches.

Moved and aroused by this warmth, and by Shontay's pliant, yielding mouth, Laura barely realized that she had raised her hand and let her fingertips run very gently across Shontay's cheek. But Shontay opened her eyes.

"No touching," she said softly. "You promised."

Laura dropped her hand. "You're right. I did. I forgot."

Now they had broken off the kiss and needed to start it again. Shontay looked at Laura, unwilling to resume it herself. Laura smiled and moved her mouth back into the position it had occupied when Shontay had spoken, now for the first time flicking just the tip of her tongue into the crease formed by Shontay's closed lips. Surprisingly, Shontay parted them a little, not enough to let Laura's tongue slip inside, but enough to encourage her.

Ever patient, her hot blood beginning to surge through her body, Laura teased Shontay's half-parted lips with the tip of her tongue, expressively moving her mouth against them too. She tried to communicate telepathically with the girl, beaming her feelings at Shontay, reassuring her, verbally caressing her too, but silently. I think you are so lovely, Shontay . . . so much lovelier than I had thought . . . so soft and luminous now with your hair down around your face . . . so afraid of a little warmth and so scared of your feelings. I would just love to kiss every bit of you . . . all of your long, smooth body. Wouldn't you like me to do that? Wouldn't you like me, for example, to kiss you between your thighs? Wouldn't you like me to kiss that pretty little bottom of yours? Would you let me? I could make you feel so good.

This kiss had now gone on quite a while, and Laura marveled that neither of them grew impatient enough to push it further, or in Shontay's case, perhaps, to break it off. She likes it, Laura realized. She pushed a little harder with her tongue, trying to get it inside Shontay's mouth. Almost imperceptibly, Shontay's full lips parted more, then even more, and soon Laura's tongue was sliding in past her teeth.

This was a penetration of sorts, and both of them knew it. Laura could even feel a faint, very faint shudder in Shontay as she felt Laura's tongue enter her mouth. Her own tongue did not meet Laura's. Passive and yielding, she did nothing to stop Laura's probing tongue, though Laura could feel her breathing accelerate.

After about half a minute, Shontay slowly pulled back, breaking off the kiss. She was breathing more heavily, her eyes slightly glassy. She gave Laura a tight, nervous smile.

"I liked that," Laura breathed, smiling back. "Let's sit down and do some more of it."

If you enjoyed this sample then look for **The Laura and Shontay Chronicles Complete Series.**

Also by this Author:

Deep Excavation

Chocolate Sandwich

Post-Game Specials

A Breach in the Preacher's Daughter

Deeply Detoured

The Rich Bitch Itch

"Hard" Competition

Little Rich Girls Go First

Superior Playmate

Spicing Up a Business Conference

Green Minds Lead to Colorful Results

Dirty Acquaintance

Menage a Trois

Provisional Test

Holiday Treat and Heat

Sex on the 46th Floor

Sneak, Peek and Squeak

Distance Leads to a Sexual Marathon

Confessions and Steamy Clinches

Screams of Pleasure

Caught in the Act

Pull My Hair and Make Me Come!

The Emperor Wants Your Pussy!

Three on a Bed

No One Can Replace You

Lock Up the Dogs!

Not While She's Looking

Blindfold Me and Lick Me All Over

Do Me Up the Ass Please

Ride 'Em Cowgirl

I'm Going to Come So Fast

Gina Loves the Dick

Bathtub Sex With Frankie

Spanking Gina's Beautiful Black Ass

Finding Marni's G-Spot

Naked and Horny in the Woods

Marni Wants It Hard, Ashley Wants It Wet

Water My Ficus

Deshona Chronicles Compilation

Kissing Marni's Mom

Shagging Shamika's Aunt

Laura and Gail Chronicles

From the Author

WANT FREE COPIES OF MY BOOKS?
Just visit my blog and download free copies of my books:
http://miranda-mars.awesomeauthors.org/

If you'd like to give me comments or suggestions to any of my books, feel free to shoot me an email at:
miranda_mars@awesomeauthors.org.

Check my page on Amazon and my blog for Updates and interesting info.

Author Central - http://amzn.to/14wSFHW

If you enjoyed any of my books then please share the love and click like on my books in Amazon.

If you write me a review and send me an email I will send you a free book, or many.
(Just know that these emails are filtered by my publisher.)

Good news is always welcome.

One Last Thing, For Kindle Readers...

When you turn the page, Kindle will give you the opportunity to rate this book and share your thoughts on Facebook and Twitter. If you enjoyed my writings, would you please take a few seconds to let your friends know about it? Because... when they enjoy they will be grateful to you and so will I.

Thank You!

Miranda Mars
Miranda_mars@awesomeauthors.org

About the Author

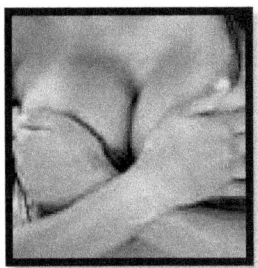

Miranda Mars lives with her cats and her exercise machines with her "special" friend in a suburb in San Francisco. Here is where she lavishly spends scribbling erotica for your, and her own, amusement.

She is especially attracted to dark-skinned women, and uses them as the lovers of the main characters in the stories she writes. She says they're just so hot! So dark-skinned women, BEWARE! :-)

Her stories are also surprisingly VERY ENTERTAINING for MEN!

www.ingramcontent.com/pod-product-compliance
Lightning Source LLC
Chambersburg PA
CBHW061457170626
46811CB00004B/1561